P9-DGY-738

Deck the Halls

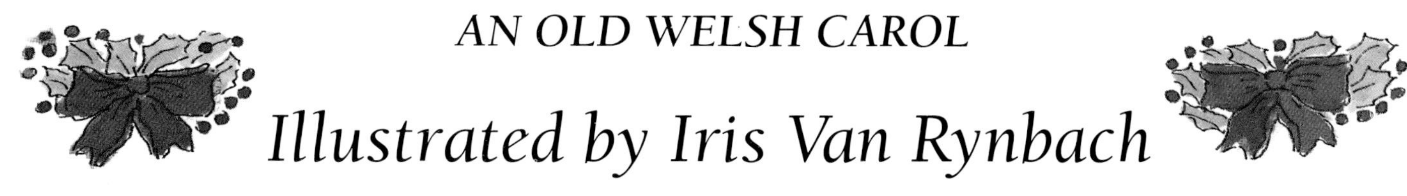

AN OLD WELSH CAROL

Illustrated by Iris Van Rynbach

Boyds Mills Press

For Amelie and Cecily—I. V. R.

Published by Bell Books
Boyds Mills Press, Inc.
A Highlights Company
815 Church Street
Honesdale, Pennsylvania 18431
Printed in Mexico

Publisher Cataloging-in-Publication Data
Van Rynbach, Iris.
Deck the halls / Iris Van Rynbach.—1st ed.
[24]p. : col. ill. ; cm.
Summary : An illustrated version of the traditional Christmas carol.
ISBN 1-56397-603-X
1. Christmas music—Juvenile literature. [1. Christmas music.] I. Title.
783.6 [E]-dc20 1996 AC CIP
Library of Congress Catalog Card Number 95-83430

First edition, 1996
Book designed by Jean Krulis
The text of this book is set in 33-point Berkeley Bold Italic.
The illustrations are done in watercolors.

10 9 8 7 6 5 4 3 2 1

Deck the halls with boughs of holly,

Fa-la-la-la-la-la-la-la-la.

'Tis the season to be jolly,
Fa-la-la-la-la-la-la-la-la.

Don we now our gay apparel,
Fa-la-la-la-la-la-la-la-la.

Troll the ancient Yuletide carol,

Fa-la-la-la-la-la-la-la-la.

See the blazing Yule before us,
Fa-la-la-la-la-la-la-la-la.

Strike the harp and join the chorus,
Fa-la-la-la-la-la-la-la-la.

Follow me in merry measure,
Fa-la-la-la-la-la-la-la-la.
While I tell of Yuletide treasure,
Fa-la-la-la-la-la-la-la-la.

isical Instruments

Fast away the old year passes,
Fa-la-la-la-la-la-la-la-la.

Hail the new, ye lads and lasses,
Fa-la-la-la-la-la-la-la-la.

Sing we joyous all together,

Fa-la-la-la-la-la-la-la-la.

Heedless of the wind
and weather,

Fa-la-la-la-la-la-la-la-la.

Deck the Halls

Old Welsh Carol

Arranged by J. W. Bradley

1. Deck the halls with boughs of hol - ly, Fa la la la la la la la la.
2. See the bla - zing Yule be - fore us, Fa la la la la la la la la.

'Tis the sea - son to be jol - ly, Fa la la la la la la la la.
Strike the harp and join the cho - rus, Fa la la la la la la la la.

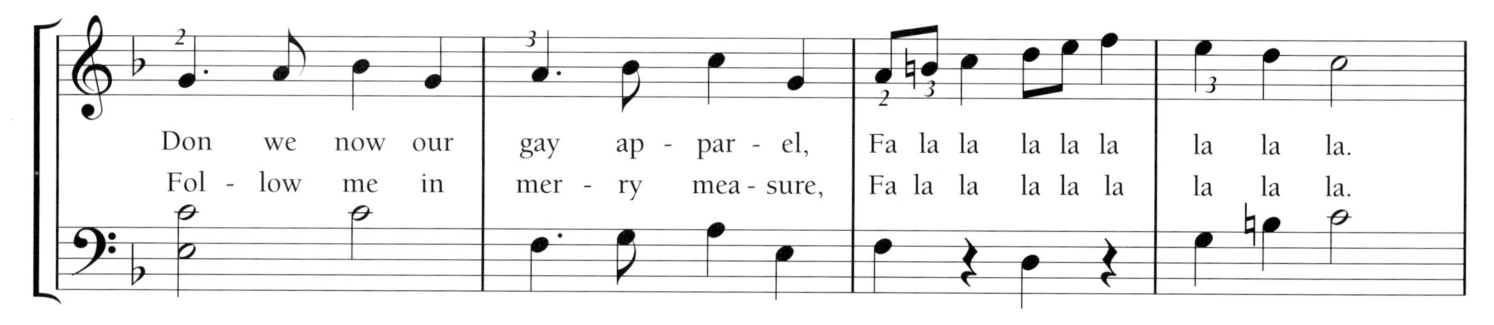

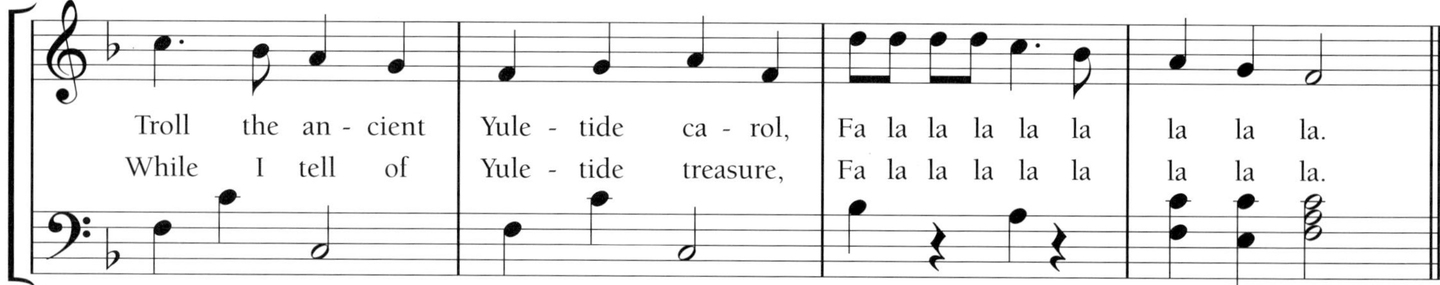

3. Fast away the old year passes
Hail the new, ye lads and lasses
Sing we joyous all together
Heedless of the wind and weather